For Elliot xx

LITTLE TIGER PRESS LTD,
an imprint of the Little Tiger Group
1 Coda Studios, 189 Munster Road, London SW6 6AW
www.littletiger.co.uk

First published in Great Britain 2019

Text and illustrations by Joanne Partis
Text and illustrations copyright © Little Tiger Press 2019
Joanne Partis has asserted her right to be identified as the
author and illustrator of this work under the Copyright,
Designs and Patents Act, 1988

A CIP catalogue record for this book is available from
the British Library

Printed in China • LTP/1400/2647/0219

2 4 6 8 10 9 7 5 3 1

Oh NO, BEAR!

JOANNE PARTIS

LITTLE TIGER

LONDON

Hello, Bear!
Bear has woken up
and he is HUNGRY!

"I have an important thing to do today," thinks Bear.

"Now, what is it . . . ?"

Bear's list of things to do today.
1. Eat
2. Sleep

A lovely smell is drifting through the forest.
It is **very** distracting!

Sniff . . .

Sniff . . .

Bear has a clever nose. It is very good at following delicious smells.

And delicious smells like this can mean only one thing.
FOOD!

"Hello, Bear!" It's Rabbit and her friends.
They're very busy digging up carrots.

What an **enormous** pile!
"Try a carrot!" offers Rabbit.
"Well, if you insist," says Bear.

"This one is good," thinks Bear, having a nibble. "And this one is particularly . . .

. . . CARROTY.

And I'll just have a little try of this one . . ."

OH NO,
BEAR!

Oh dear.

The wheelbarrow of carrots
seems to be empty.

"Where are our carrots?" asks Rabbit.
"We spent ages picking them!"

"I'm sorry," mumbles Bear. "I only meant to have
a little taste."

Bear looks at the field of carrots waiting to
be picked. But before he can think of a very
helpful idea, his nose begins to tingle.

Another lovely smell is drifting past.

Bear forgets all about helping poor Rabbit
and sets off after it.

Careful where you're treading, Bear!

"Hello, Bear!" says Squirrel. She's been very busy picking delicious acorns with her friends.

To a bear with a hungry tummy and a clever nose, acorns smell fantastic!

"Would you like to help us pick some?" asks Squirrel. "You can try some, too!"

"Yes please!" says Bear eagerly. "Mmmm," he munches happily. It is hard to say much with a large mouthful of tasty acorns.

"Mmmmm,

MMMmm,

MMMMM!"

OH NO, BEAR!

Oh dear. It's happened again.

"You were supposed to fill up the baskets,
not your tummy!" grumbles Squirrel.
   It is amazing quite how many acorns will
fit in a hungry bear's tummy.
   "I'm sorry," says Bear. "Maybe I could help
you find some more acorn trees?" Bear looks
around but . . .

Sniff . . .

It's very hard to concentrate when . . .

Sniff . . .

Yet another tempting
smell comes drifting
through the trees.

"SLOW
DOWN,
BEAR!"

"Hello, Bear," waves Beaver. "Look at the lovely fish I've caught for my tea."

"I won't eat Beaver's fish," Bear thinks to himself.
He is sure that he can resist this time.

"Have a little taste if you like!" shouts Beaver.

Oh dear.

Bear has accidentally eaten Beaver's fish.

"That was supposed to be my tea!" moans Beaver.

"I was trying so hard not to eat it," says Bear sadly. "I wonder if maybe there are more fish in the river?"

Bear jumps in . . .

SPLASH!

"No," he splutters. "None in here."

Bear can't find any fish at all. Where have they all gone?

"I'm sorry, Beaver," says Bear gloomily. "I ate the only fish in the whole river."

Time to be off, Bear thinks.

Poor Bear. Things really haven't gone right today at all.

"I shouldn't have eaten Beaver's fish," says Bear to himself, rubbing his rather large belly.

"Or Squirrel's acorns.

OR Rabbit's carrots."

What if Bear's friends are angry with him? And what if they go hungry all winter?

"I will go straight back to my cave to do some extra hard thinking," yawns Bear, suddenly feeling very sleepy.

"I will think up a way to make all my friends happy again."

But when he gets home, Bear can't squeeze
his tummy through the front door.
Bear is very confused.

He's sure he lived here this morning!

Poor Bear.

He is wet and tired and full, and now his house is
the wrong size too!

He squeezes and wriggles but it's no good. He just
won't fit in.

"I'm stuck!" he cries.

He really is a sad bear.

But who's this coming through
the forest?

"Hello, Bear!" call his friends.
"We've come to thank you."

"You dug up all these carrots,"
says Rabbit.

"And bumped the trees to make the
acorns fall," says Squirrel.

"And you caught all the fish in the river!"
says Beaver.

Bear waves his legs in reply. He feels a little silly
as his friends have to chat to his bottom.

"Now let us help you!" says Rabbit kindly.

They heave and
push until . . .

POP!

Bear is in! It is the right house after all!
   "Thank you, everyone," smiles Bear sleepily.
"Did I really help all of you even though I ate
your food?"

"You really did," says Beaver.
    "And you always eat a lot when it's
time to hibernate!" adds Squirrel.
    "Hibernate!" yawns Bear happily.
"That's the important thing I have
to remember . . . to . . . do."

Goodnight, Bear.
See you in the spring!

Bear's list of things to do today.
1. Eat
2. Sleep